I'm Reading About

ARIZONA

The Grand Canyon State!

GALLOPADE

by Carole Marsh

Printed and Manufactured in Peachtree City, GA., USA
www.gallopade.com

Book design: John Hanson

Editorial manager: Janice Baker

Arizona is a great state.
It is one of a kind.

What makes Arizona special?
Let's read about it
and see!

NATIVE AMERICANS

Who lived in Arizona first?

Native Americans did!

They moved around to find food.
They hunted for animals to eat.
They fished in Arizona's rivers.
They gathered fruits and seeds and nuts.

EXPLORERS

Father Marcos de Niza came to Arizona in 1539.
He traveled to Arizona from Mexico.

Marcos de Niza explored the area and claimed it for Spain.

He and his men were looking for cities of gold!

N
NE
E
SE
S
SW
W
NW

HISTORY

Spanish missionaries came to Arizona from Mexico. They came to bring Christianity to the Indians.

Father Kino founded the San Xavier del Bac Mission in 1692. A beautiful church was built there about 100 years later. It is located near the city of Tucson.

There are beautiful paintings, carvings, and statues inside the church!

Mission

STATEHOOD

Arizona was the 48th state to join the United States of America!

Isn't it great,
to be a state!
I bet Arizona
could hardly wait!

Arizona became a state in 1912.

Arizona
The 48th State
Here we are!

FLAG

I am the state flag.
I was adopted in 1917.

What colors am I?
Blue. Red. Yellow.

Look at me.
What else do you see?

I fly high over the state of Arizona!

CAPITAL

Say hello to Phoenix,
the capital city of Arizona!

There is an important building in Phoenix.
It is the State Capitol.
Arizona's laws are made there!

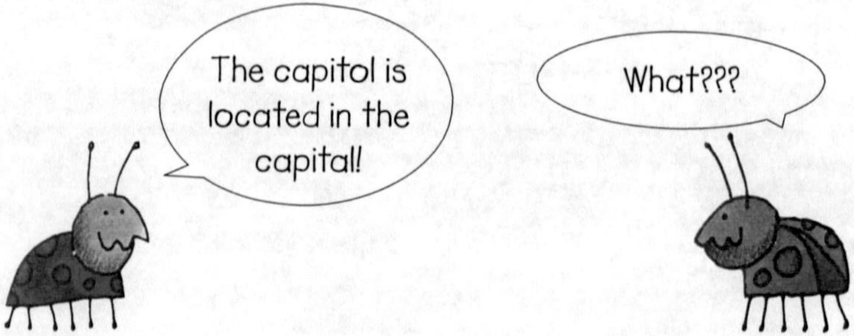

Capitol
Phoenix
Capital

SEAL

I am a seal,
but I am not the State Seal.
If I were, I would be very important.
I would be stamped on many official papers.
(Ouch, that might hurt!)

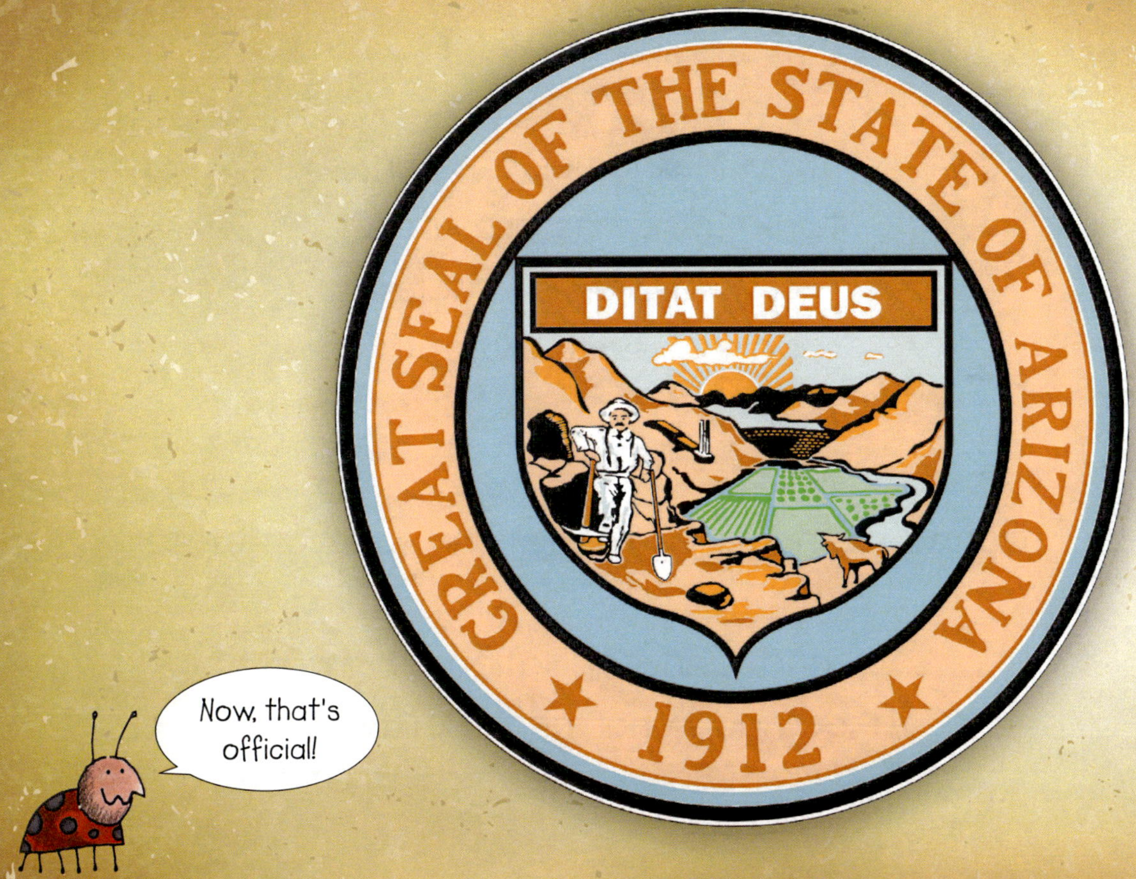
GREAT SEAL OF THE STATE OF ARIZONA
DITAT DEUS
1912
Now, that's official!

NICKNAME

State nicknames are fun!
State nicknames are great!
They share fun facts
about each state!

Arizona's nickname is "The Grand Canyon State."

Grand Canyon National Park
is located in northern Arizona!

The Grand Canyon State

BORDERS

Look at Arizona.
Arizona is in a region called "the Southwest."

Arizona directly borders four other states.
It also borders the country of Mexico.
Find Arizona and its neighbors on the map!

Borders

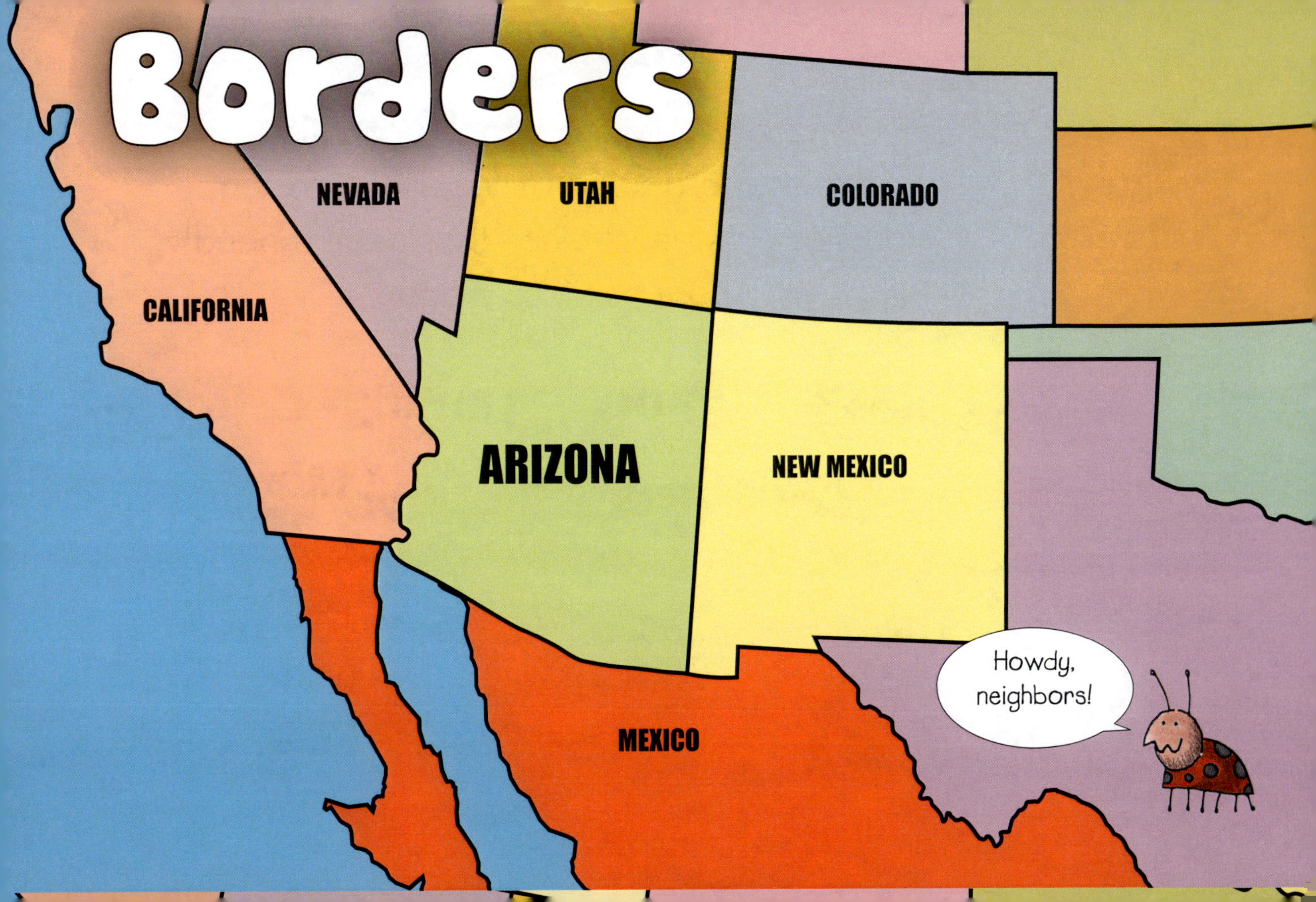
NEVADA
UTAH
COLORADO
CALIFORNIA
ARIZONA
NEW MEXICO
MEXICO
Howdy, neighbors!

COUNTIES

Arizona is divided into 15 counties.
Counties are a form of local government.
Counties provide services that people need!
Those services include:

Schools **Parks** **Libraries** **Police**
Firefighters **and More!**

Counties

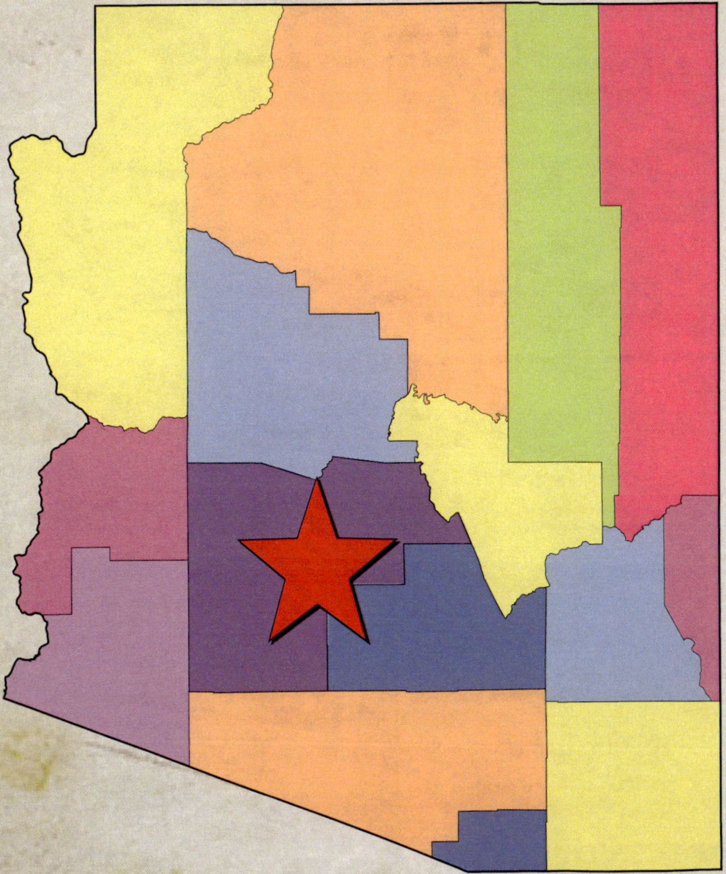

Many famous people

Geronimo

Apache Indian leader

Frank Luke

First airman to receive the Medal of Honor for bravery

Cesar Chavez

Farm worker leader who founded a labor union

PEOPLE

call our state home!

Sandra Day O'Connor

First female Associate Justice of the U.S. Supreme Court

John McCain

U.S. Senator and prisoner of war in the Vietnam War

Kerri Strug

Gymnast who won a gold medal in the 1996 Olympic Games

Cactus Wren

BIRD

I am the state bird, and I fly
over Arizona, proud and high.

As I fly, up in the sky,
I flap my wings to tell you "Hi!"

The Arizona state bird is the Cactus Wren.

Saguaro Cactus Blossom

FLOWER

I am the Saguaro Cactus Blossom.
I am the state flower.

I grow where it's warm and sunny.
I bloom in spring and summer.
I help make Arizona beautiful!

Look at me! Smell me!
But don't touch the sharp thorns!

Palo Verde

TREE

I am a Palo Verde—I'm the state tree.
Arizona's deserts are where to find me.

My roots run deep, they keep me strong.
I can live for hundreds of years—that's very long.

I stand up straight, big and tall.
Don't climb too high—it would hurt to fall!

Two-tailed Swallowtail Butterfly

INSECT

I am the Two-tailed Swallowtail Butterfly.
I am the state insect.

I flit and I fly from flower to flower.
I am looking for nectar to drink.

Look at my beautiful wings.
What colors do you see?

Deserts

Let's go to the desert!

The desert is dry.
It hardly ever rains.

Temperatures are hot during the day,
but cool off at night!

Arizona's deserts are home to many animals:

Scorpions **Snakes** **Hawks** **Coyotes** **Tarantulas** **and More!**

DESERTS

Mountains

Arizona's mountains are the place to be.
Hiking, fishing, camping—
fun for you and me.

If you were to climb
to the top of a tree,
you'd have a very nice view to see!

Rivers

RIVERS

Arizona has many rivers.
People like to use rivers for boating and fishing!

This habitat is home to many animals:

Birds Deer Snakes Frogs Fish and More!

The Colorado River is an important source of water for Arizona!

Monument Valley

Monument Valley is a cluster of buttes!
A butte is a tall hill with a flat top.
The buttes in Monument Valley are reddish brown.
They tower above the desert floor.

Monument Valley is on the border of Arizona and Utah.
Many Western movies have been filmed there!

Arizona Crops

Cotton

Hay

Lettuce

Melons

AGRICULTURE

Arizona has many farms.
Why?
Because Arizona has good soil and a warm climate!

Some of the top crops grown in Arizona are:

Cotton **Hay** **Lettuce** **Melons**

Hey!
Don't forget about me!
Arizona farmers raise lots of cattle, too!
Moooooooooo!

Sports in Arizona

Baseball! Basketball! Football!
Arizona has it all.

Whether you like to watch or play,
You are sure to have a ball!

Cardinals **Diamondbacks**

Coyotes **Suns**

Sun Devils

Wildcats

& More!

Arizona: Home of the Grand Canyon

The Grand Canyon is in Arizona!
It is a deep canyon with steep walls.
The walls of the Grand Canyon show many layers of rock.
The canyon is more than one mile deep!

The Colorado River flows through the bottom of the Grand Canyon.

GLOSSARY

canyon: a deep gorge, often with a river running through it

climate: weather conditions in an area over a long period of time

cluster: a group of similar things close together

habitat: a place where plants or animals naturally live

labor union: an organization of employees formed to protect workers' rights

laws: rules made by the government

nectar: a sweet liquid produced by plants, especially flowers

region: an area that has similar characteristics